His thoughts...

Her thighs

"His thoughts are always between her thighs..."

BetrayalBooks.com Presents

His thoughts...

Her thighs

BetrayalBooks.com

Please visit my website at www.BetrayalBooks.com

Printed in the United States of America

First printing: June 2011

ISBN-13: 978-0-9828628-0-3

Front cover design: Waltham Park Design Group

Dedicated to JuNiPh…with love!!!

Warning:

This book is not for the faint of heart. If you have any of the following conditions, please put this book down and run for your life!

Conditions:

Weak heart

Jealousy issues

Holier than thou

Married and have a hard time accepting that married men sleep around

Have a problem with misspelling, mispunctuations or other proof reading issues because this book is self-published and I had no idea what I was doing and you're not okay with that...

THIS BOOK AIN'T FOR YOU!

Prologue

For most of you bitches, fairy tales do come true. Most of you as little girls dreamt of the big white wedding and the beautiful house with the picket fence. Yeah you know that fantasy. That fantasy with the great husband, 2.5 kids, a dog and the nice ass car sitting out in the driveway. Yeah that one!! Well, that wasn't a dream of mine. That shit never existed in my world.

I never heard of that particular fairy tale until I was grown. Once I grew up and was able to be around us so called "women" I thought it was fascinating yet foolish to see how desperate some of these women were to get married. Ughhhh…but for me I never wanted that shit.

As a child, I saw the struggles of what my parents went through. I saw my father on heroine and he used to beat the shit out of my mother. And my mother…apparently she thought that she was born to be his punching bag. And outside of the beatings, we were just poor as hell.

Anyway, that shit is neither here nor there. Just to sum all the bullshit up:

1. We were dirt poor.
2. We moved around a lot like gypsies.
3. My siblings and I didn't grow up together.
4. My mother was depressed.
5. My daddy died.
6. I was ugly as hell growing up.
7. My teeth were fucked up.
8. I got dumped at both of my proms. (Yes both!)

So that's pretty much it for my childhood. But luckily I got a job, got my teeth fixed and was able to fix myself up. And without further ado, here are their thoughts about what's in between my thighs....

Thanking God for some great pussy,

Delilah

The FUNeral...

Thomas

1

(Sitting in church)…

I don't know what's come over me. Right now I'm at my dad's funeral and I can't believe that he's dead. I'm trying not to cry right now because I need to be strong for my family. My wife and our 3 children are sitting next to me and I can't help but to think about the day when they will bury me.

But right now I can't think about that. I can't show my children that I'm distraught and I don't want them to view me as being weak. So I'm going to raise my head up and look at my dad lying in his casket and take this shit like a man.

While I'm trying to be strong and not break down all over this damn place, I've just seen one pretty ass woman. She's beyond pretty. She's beautiful! Not only is she beautiful, but she's grown now and I barely recognize her. She just came down the aisle and took her seat but she's dressed in all white which is different for a funeral.

But if I may be honest with you, she's **FUCKING HOT!** And she's such a distraction in my mind right now that I can't even possibly think about my dad. I'm shaking my head right now because she's now an adult and I really want her…bad.

I know I shouldn't feel this way, but I can't help myself. I'm still watching her and although she's crying, somehow she just managed to look over her shoulder at me and she said, without verbally saying, "I love you!" as I read her sweet tender brown lips. Damnit man!

I can't believe that this little brown honey drop loves me already but I don't think that it's the way that I love her. I'm getting kind of nervous so I'm going to just look down at my hands so I can think about my dad. I'm just hoping that my wife is thinking that I'm anxious about my dad's funeral.

3

But right now I need God because how I'm feeling about that woman is just wrong…damn wrong. My beautiful and loving wife is sitting next to me and I'm having heart palpitations and sexual thoughts about another woman. I wish I could scream but what in the hell do I do now???

(Funeral is over)….

Okay the funeral is over and my father is still lying in his blue casket lifeless. They're giving the flower girls the flowers and I'm still sitting here thinking about her. But no matter what, I will get through this. So now I have to leave and pick my dad up with the other pallbearers but before I walk up there, I must take a look at her…one more time.

(Quick gaze)…

She's still over there crying…her and my grandmother. I haven't seen my grandmother in a long time and it's been forever since I've seen her. I had no earthly idea that the little girl that I haven't seen in years would grow up to be a beauty. This woman has captivated me. (sigh)…I must go now. My father is waiting to be buried.

But she is forever in my soul. And I hope that someday, just someday perhaps that she will be sitting on my………. ”Honey you need to go up
there. The other pallbearers are waiting on you.” my wife said as she interrupted my thoughts. There she goes…always interrupting my damn thoughts. Damn. Let me go…it's time to go bury my dad.

(An hour later…after the burial…)

My dad is in his final resting place and everyone is back at the church eating. Since I wasn't able to see my grandmother at the funeral in the church, its best that I go speak to her now.

(Talking to my grandmother)…

So right now I'm with my grandmother and guess who just walked up to me? Yes…the lady in white has come over and as nervous as I am right now, she decides to give me a nice hug. Damn…she feels so damn good and smells so nice that I could just eat her up….literally.

And now I've noticed that my body is starting to feel some type of sexual arousal as she's hugging me but I must hold it in. I can't let my dick get on hard. Not here, not now, not **EVER!!!** Damn. Why her God? Why her? Hmmm…why now?

She's finally let me go and we (me her and my grandmother) talked for a few more minutes. Now they've gone to their table to eat and I'm going to go sit at the table with my wife and kids. I just can't believe that this shit is happening. And I was truly enjoying holding her warm body against mine.

I want her so bad, but I must keep this secret with me. I can never tell another soul how I am feeling about this woman. I will do my best to hold my feelings inside of me hopefully until the day that I die. Because I can't ever tell anyone that this woman that I've fallen in love with at first sight is my **half-sister**.

After the funeral: the visit

7

(Hanging up the phone)…

Wow! My half-sister just called and she's on her way over here. What the fuck?! Why am I so nervous and giddy at the same time? Damnit man! She's my sister and I'm acting like I have a crush on her. But duh. I do have a crush on her but only I know that.

Okay let me get it together. She said she will be here in about an hour. **(Looking at my watch)** That gives me enough time to get the living room together and let my wife know that she's coming. I am so excited. I haven't seen her since the funeral and that's been about 2 weeks now. Plus this will give her a chance to get to know my wife and kids.

(Phone rings again)…

I know that this can't be her again. **(Looking down at the phone)**…Shit!!! Why the fuck is she calling me ? Now?? This ain't a good time for me to talk and I really don't want to speak to her even if I could. Fuck it! **(Starting to panic)…**Let me calm down. I'm losing my cool and my wife is watching me so I gotta play it cool. I'm sending this call straight to voicemail. **(Pushed button)…**

"Honey…Are you okay?" she asked. "Why didn't you answer that? (So I have a choice…tell her that my other woman was calling and then she will get upset and then I would have to choke hold her ass or I can lie right now and avoid all the violence…so I'm going to lie to her as usual).

"That was a business call that I didn't want to take and the call before that one was my half-sister. She's on her way to visit us" I replied. "Really?" she responded with a smile on her face. That lets me know right there that she has no clue that I want to fuck my half-sister. "That's good. I didn't think that you two would see each other again after the funeral."

I really don't know if I should respond to her statement so I'm going to keep quiet. I just told her that I was going to take a shower and help her straighten up the house once I got out. "You seem to be jumpy or anxious. Your sister doesn't make you nervous?" she said as she looked at me...straight into my eyes as if she was fishing for something. "It seems like you've been acting strange ever since she called you. Calm down!"

Now her clueless ass is laughing. If she only knew why I'm acting nervous she wouldn't be laughing…her ass would be crying. So I'm just gonna shake my head and laugh with her ass. Ha, ha bitch…that's what I want to say but I can't…she's my wife. But I can think it.

10

The truth of the matter is that I'm very excited that my fine ass half-sister is on her way over to my house to see me!!! Yes sir!!! I just can't wait to see her again. I want to see her brown thick ass…"Oh by the way, why do you call her your half-sister? She's still your sister regardless of the fact that the both of you have different mothers. So just say your sister or better yet just say her name. I know who she is" she said while interrupting my corrupt thoughts about my half-sister. Shit…

"I'm going to wash my dick…," I said to my wife (in my head). She's too fucking prim and proper for me to talk to her like that. "I'm going to go take a quick shower so you just keep on cooking because I'm hungry" I said and kissed her on the forehead. Sometimes I really just want to tell her to suck my dick but…never mind. That shit never happens anymore. I'm headed to the bathroom…

11

(About an hour or so later…doorbell rings)…

"I got it!" as I yelled to my wife. It's taking everything in me to not run or skip to that door like a fucking bitch but I'm trying to keep my composure. Thanking God right now that my wife is in the kitchen so she can't see my face. As much as I'm attracted to my half-sister right now, I really wish that I wasn't. But for whatever reason, which I don't know why, God has put me in this situation. Anyway, let me open the door and let her fine chocolate ass in. **(Opening the door with a smile on the outside and laughing hard on the inside).**

"Hi big brother!!!!" she said as she walked through my front door. God she is so fine that it's just fucking ridiculous. The first thing that she does is embrace me in her arms and as much as I don't want to let her go, I feel the need to. My dick is swelling up and I don't want her to feel it so I have to get her off of me. "Hi baby girl! Come on in and welcome to our home!" My dick is about to explode…literally.

"Wow! You have a nice place", she said as she brought her fine ass in my house. "And you have one helluva an ass" is what I wanted to say but I replied with "Thank you. It's okay but come in and make yourself comfortable" as I escorted her to the family room. "Can I get you a drink or some dick?" I thought to myself but I just asked her if I could get her something to drink. She declined…the drink. Dick hasn't been offered…yet.

Anyway, we've just sat down and are continuing to talk. While she's talking, I'm just trying fucking hard to stay focused. I'm looking directly in her eyes while she's speaking to me but this shit is harder than my dick right now. And she's making it hard for me to stay focused on what she's saying.

Let me tell you what my half-sister is wearing. She's wearing these tight ass pussy print white pants with a white tank top. And to really make things worse, the top of her tits are hanging out of her shirt and I just wish that one of her golden brown nipples would just slide out and land right between my lips. I really just want to rip her shirt off and play with her breasts…with my tongue. I'm nasty.

13

Now don't get me wrong, I'm not a real shoe man, but the heels that she's wearing, makes me want to lick her ankles. Part of me wants to believe that she's dressed like this to turn me on but the other part, naw…I don't think she sees me in a sexual manner. I really feel like screaming. She is so fucking fine!! Why God?? Why are you torturing me like this??!! Is it because I've cheated on my wife already?

I can't help but to keep watching her breasts. I just want to pinch them, hold them, caress them and most all just pour some syrup on them and just lick her nips. I know that I'm sick…sitting over here lusting after my half-sister like this. I'm so damn lost for words right now that the only thing that I can come up with to say is, "White must be your favorite color?" I asked. "Why yes it is!" she replied. Before I could reply, my wife decides to interrupt our conversation.

"Hi sister-in-law!" my wife yells as she comes in the family room with a big ass kool-aid smile but at the same time fucking up my fantasy. My half-sister is standing up and now she's turning around to hug my wife. I see nothing but a juicy ass right in front of my face and she's not wearing any panties…my half-sister isn't. I can tell.

(Smiling)…

"Hi! How are you? Great to see you again!" my half-sister responds. My dick is standing up…literally. "So good to see you again and I love your shoes!!" my wife says to her. And now all of my children walk into the room and the conversation has begun…without me. My wife and half-sister are chatting it up and I can't be any happier because while they are talking, I'm sitting here staring and fantasizing about her…not my wife. I feel so guilty but yet so good at the same time. I want her…now.

While they are over there chit chatting, I'm sitting here with a semi-rock hard dick and pretending like I'm engaged with what they are saying, but I could give a rats ass about their conversation. I'm just mesmerized just by watching my half-sister's face and her movements. She is so fucking beautiful and she has the prettiest skin that I've ever seen. Her skin is chocolate brown and smooth…no blemishes or cracks.

Just fucking flawless!! I just want to go run my hands across her face and give her all of this dick. Speaking of my dick, it's now making me focus on her lips. I can see her sucking my dick. I wish that you could see her lips. They are small but just right. She's wearing a little lip gloss and when she smiles...damn. I just saw myself tonguing her down.

Okay so right now I'm looking at her neck because I couldn't just keep staring at her lips. And her neck is beautiful just like the rest of her. If I had several wishes then one of them would be that I could be Dracula for a day. I would just lovingly bite the hell out of her!!! Good God Almighty! **LET ME STOP FANTASIZING ABOUT HER!!!** I need to go to the bathroom.

"Excuse me for a moment" and I'm leaving. My wife is talking her to death but I don't think that they care if I'm there or not. I'm headed to the bathroom to jack my dick off. It won't take too long. I'm used to jacking off fast. I'll be back.

(In the bathroom, sitting on the toilet jacking off…sweating…thinking about her…naked…on her knees…sucking my dick…nutting in her mouth…her swallowing…and everything else imaginable)…

I need prayer!!! I can't believe that I'm in my own bathroom…sitting on my throne…jacking my dick off because of my long lost ass half-sister. This shit is crazy!!! Never in a million years would I have thought that I would be doing some shit like this but I know that her pussy is really good! I want to fuck her so bad but right now fucking her in my head is worth it. Damnit man…I'm about to cum. Be right back…

(10 minutes later)… Ahhhhhhhhhh!!!! I feel so much better and I came…hard! And yes I washed myself up including my hands. (Smiling)..Now I'm back in the family room with my wife and half-sister. I feel so fucking relieved. Now I can actually talk to her without my dick rising. Thank God for masturbation.

17

Speaking of thanking God, my wife has finally shut her damn mouth and she's gone back into the kitchen. And the kids are outside playing which leaves me and my half-sister here…alone…to talk. I'm still in awe…thanks dad. You did a fine job making this one.

"Well. How have you been?" she asks me. "I've really been craving your hot black ass but I've been okay" is what I thought but what I said was "I've been okay. Hanging in there. I have no complaints except that I'm missing dad. What about you?" wishing that she could sit on my face and let me lick her fat pussy. (By the way, she's talking to me with her legs spread wide open…I just want to give that cat some milk.)

"I've been okay. Just living and taking care of Big Mama. You know that you really need to check in on her from time to time" she says. I agreed with her and we continued to talk while I continue to visualize how many different ways that I could make her cum.

So we're still talking and then she just blurts out, "I want to go out to a bar or something tonight. Can you hang out with your little sister tonight or do you have plans? I know it's kind of last minute but I would love to hang out with you…catch up on our lives." My heart is racing and my balls are getting heated up just thinking about being alone with her. So I replied, "Let me check with the old ball and chain about that! We didn't have any plans."

Now we're laughing as I'm walking into the kitchen to ask permission to go out with my little "sister". Ain't nothing little about her except her lips…on her face. I know my wife won't mind but for us men, it's best to just ask to keep down the confusion at home. I'm asking now. "Sure. No problem but don't have too much fun!" she says. "Naw. I just want to spend some time with her and play catch up"…smiling as I'm giving her a big hug.

"Well go! The kids and I will be fine. Dinner will be waiting for you so you two go ahead and have a great time!" she says. She's walking me out of the kitchen and she says her goodbyes to my half-sister. I'm gathering my keys right now and I'm at the front door about to leave. "I won't have too much fun but I'll be home before you know it. See you later. Love you" as I kiss her on her forehead.

I must say that I have a great wife. She's an awesome mother and truly a great friend. The only thing that's not right in our relationship is our sex life. Well, let me rephrase that…it's her sex life. After she had the kids, well her pussy just ain't the same. It's not as tight as it used to be and to be honest, she never really liked having sex. And she sucks dick like she's eating rocks. She's so bad that I just told her that I could live without her giving me head. No head is better than bad head. I had hoped that the sex would get better, but my hope is dead.

I love her but that's why I had the other woman on the side but that's another story. Yeah, that's the phone call that I got earlier. She's mad as hell. I've been trying to cut her ass off since my dad's funeral but she doesn't understand that I don't want to see her anymore. Anyway, my half-sister and I have said our goodbyes to my family and we have gotten the hell on. We both decided that we will drop her car off and I will drive to the club. So now we're headed to her apartment.

(Smiling)…

Her apartment

I'm sitting in her bathroom…on her throne…torn between tears of joy and tears of "I done fucked up now"! (sighing) I feel like shit, but good shit. It's this type of dumb shit that you do and you don't regret doing it while you're doing it until it's over and then you think about what the fuck you've done so now you can't fix it type of shit. Yeah…it's like that.

But this is something that I must think about like right now and just ponder on what the hell just happened….in her bed, on her floor, on her table, in her kitchen and again in her bed. Oh God!!! The thoughts, the memories of my half-sister…naked! I'm just reviewing the moments in my head so please be patient with me:

23

Somewhere in between dropping off my sister's car and going to the club, we **never ever** made it to the bar. I followed my sister home to drop off her car and when we got to the apartment, she came to my car door and asked me to come in for a minute while she changed clothes. So I said sure…no problem. I mean hell it's my sister. Even though I thought about her in a very sexual way, I didn't think that she wanted me. I thought wrong.

As I walked into her apartment, I noticed that she had a lot of different pictures with different dudes. I wanted to ask her about it but I didn't want to be nosey. Honestly, I didn't want to know. The weird part about it was I began to feel a little jealous so I had to just stop looking at her pictures. So while I was roaming around checking out her place, she went into her kitchen and fixed me a drink.

She said, "We might as well get drunk before we go to the club." And I agreed. So we started drinking margaritas and then we took some tequila shots. Then one drink led to another and we began to talk about our lives and a whole bunch of other bullshit. That was so not the right thing to do…the drinking in her apartment that is.

And the next thing I know she said "I'll be back" because she needed to change clothes again "cause I spilled my drink on my shirt." And I be damned…about 15 minutes later, she entered her living room newborn naked with some heels on. And she said the words that I had been longing to hear. She said and I quote…

"You wanna fuck?!"

MY GOD!!! I quivered because I was soooo scared to say yes because **I thought it was a sick joke. But when she sat on her couch and started to masturbate I knew that she was serious.** So before I could say yes because I was really speechless, she was already on her knees with my dick out and in her mouth. And at that very moment I had totally forgotten that she was my half-sister. Soooo…we fucked like two dogs in heat for about a good 2 hours straight.

(Back to my reality….still sitting my ass in her bathroom…on her throne…thinking)…

So now I'm still sitting here, in her bathroom, wanting to fucking cry because I feel like I've betrayed my father and I've broken some type of natural law. I mean isn't she still my sister? Don't we have our father's blood running through our veins? Shit!!! Okay let me get my ass up and get out of here and talk to her about what has happened. I'll be right back.

(An hour later…back in her bed…watching the ceiling)…

We just had sex again. What the fuck? I'm laying here butt ass naked in her bed again!!! The fucked up part about it is: **I've just had the best sex of my life with my half-sister!!!** If our dad was alive he would kill me. Shit…he would kill the both of us.

Now she's trying to kiss me on my lips but I told her that I can't kiss her again. I'm getting up from her bed and heading back to her bathroom. It seems like the bathroom is really safe for me right now. But right now I'm talking to God asking:

Dear God: Why?? Why her? Lord, I'm sorry but I need to get the fuck out of here. How can I look at her again? How do I suppose to look at myself? I'm ashamed of myself God. But I need help and I don't want to hurt her but…

27

(At the sink, washing up…looking at myself in the mirror…disgusted)…

I'm feeling sick and it's not because of the liquor. I feel so ashamed and I feel like crying but I can't. This is what I've been waiting for since the first time that I saw her at dad's funeral. I've been wanting to make love to her and I had no idea that she was attracted to me too. But this shit ain't right. This just can't be right.

(Knock, knock)…

She's knocking on the door. Fuck!!! What do I say to her outside of sorry? But the sex was GREAT!!! I knew that it would be but damn…What do I say to her??? What do I do now???

I am appalled at my very own behavior. I cannot believe that I, Delilah May Jenkins, slept with my half-brother. It was good as hell though and I harbor no regrets, but there's something that I must share with you (**yes you the reader**). I'm going to do my best to tell you this so you just hold on and follow me:

Regardless of how you may feel about me, this is what my Big Mama told me a few years ago. She said and I quote, "Mama's baby, papa maybe. Your half-brother ain't your brother." She went on to say, "His sorry ass excuse for a mother had sex with another man and lied to your daddy about him being the father. Your daddy didn't find out until a few years ago, but they never told your brother. They didn't want to hurt him so he doesn't know."

Okay so that's the story that was told to me and that's what I'm sticking by. I just hope that there's some proof to show just in case. Damn…I forgot about DNA testing but really… don't judge me. I'm only human.

(Smoking a cigarette)…

I'm still shocked but I'm glad that he's not my brother. The sex was excellent and I won't complain about that. It's just boggling my mind that he's taking it so hard. I mean he shouldn't feel too bad. It's not like we grew up together. We are practically strangers so maybe it's normal that we both were attracted to each other.

Even though that I promised Big Mama that I would never tell anyone, I think it's appropriate for me to tell him the truth. I need him to come out of the bathroom and talk to me so I can tell him that I'm not his **half-sister**.

Delilah.

Dickey: Night before wedding

31

(Loud music in the background…the smell of hot pussy is lingering in the air)…

Right now I'm here with my boys at the strip club. It's loud and there's a lot of pussy in my face, but to be honest with you, I don't want to be here. I would rather be at home with her. I'm nervous and anxious because tomorrow is my big day and I miss her already. I need another fucking drink.

(An hour and 3 drinks later)…

I'm so fucking ready to go!!! I need to see her and I can't wait until tomorrow. Shit. Well it's already midnight which is actually tomorrow but still qualifies for being today. I have to see my queen so I'm going to get one of my boys to drop me off at her house. I know they will be upset with me but I don't want to be here. But before I do that, I need to call her to make sure that it's okay to go over there. I don't want her to panic or act a fool…you know how women get all traditional before the big day.

(Phone ringing…she finally answers)…

"Baby, I know it's late but I want to be with you. I'll rather be with you than here"…I'm telling her. I love the hell out of this woman and to hell with my boys and this strip club. I know it's supposed to be my bachelor's party but fuck that. "It's okay…come on over" she said and now she's off the phone.

All the pussy in the world can't take her place. She's got the best pussy that I've **EVER** had in my life and I want to do her before the "I do's" are said. **(Putting my drink down)…**Fuck this shit!! I'm getting the hell out of here. I need her…now. **(Tapping my best man on his shoulder)…**"I'm ready to go see her…now." He's looking at me kind of funny and the shit he just told me…I feel like kicking his ass but I can't. I just have to listen to this shit, but in the end he's going to take me to see her.

33

(30 minutes later…at her front door)…

I'm nervous as hell but I can't wait to make love to my baby!!! (She finally opens the door and lets me in). Damn! She looks so damn good! I just want to eat her up. She has on this white wife beater shirt with her nipples sticking out.

And she has those big fat ass nipples with large areolas…nice and brown tits! The shirt is cut up and you can see her flat stomach. She's fucking hot! And she has on some red stilettos with no panties on. I should call her fat and juicy. LOL!

So now that I've gotten that out of the way, it's fucking hot in her house. She said that the a/c just went out today so I told her that I will get it fixed but right now I don't give a shit about the temperature of the house. I just want to ram my dick in her and make her squirt tonight.

Just give her a little something before the vows are said later on…if you know what I mean. But ummm…right now I'm about to go crazy because she just shoved me on the steps and right now at this very minute…she's taking my pants down and damn it…….she has my dick her mouth.

OOOOOOOOOOOHHHWWWWEEEE!!!!!

(Gotta go…)

(About 3 hours later and a whole lot of nutting)…

Okay, okay. Whew! We just got done fucking and right now her fine ass is taking a shower. I'm just chilling in her bed thinking about how wrong I am for coming to see her but I wanted some real pussy. And besides that, I love this woman. She's all I ever wanted and the loving is so damn good!

35

I call her Miss Sweet Pussy. Right now I'm thinking about the first time we fucked. I remember when I first put my dick in her from the back…it was so damn good. It was so good that I beat her fat juicy ass like it was a set of congos!!!

(Smiling)…If I could put her pussy in a bottle and sale it, I would be rich as hell. It's just that good…well great! And I love her just the way she is. She's smart, sexy, outgoing and funny! And she's a great mother, too. I like to think of her kids as my own because I love them too.

(Slight tear falls out of my eye)…

She's gotten back in the bed and I'm holding her. "I love you" I said to her. I know that she loves me too but today is the big day. I'm so fucking sad. It's really fucked up that I've been making love to this woman all night….. the woman of my dreams. But in about 12 hours I will be saying **"I do"** to a woman that **"I don't"** want. Damn.

Night before wedding:
Harry (best man)

37

Loud music in background

I'm really pissed the fuck off right now!!! I'm sitting here with the soon to be groom and he wants me to drop him off at his "bitch on the side" house. Me and the boys did all of this for him to come out to the strip club to have fun for his bachelor party. We are trying to get him to celebrate his last day of freedom but noooooo…Mr. Pussy Whipped wants to leave.

Fuck that! I don't want him to leave but I can't hold a grown ass man down. But let me honest here. I'm really fucking pissed off because he wants to go see Ms. Side Piece. Yeah I know I shouldn't be upset but I am. I feel like such a hater but I'm really not.

I just can't believe that my dude is getting married tomorrow and all he can think about is that other woman? Sometimes he can be so stupid and get caught up. Look at him now…over there on the phone calling her. I'm sure he's begging her for some pussy. And I'm sitting here thinking…about his side piece of pussy. She's pussy whipped me too. (Shaking my head)…She's fucking wrong for being with him. (Taking a shot of Patron)

She knows how I feel about her. Damn…I bet she's going to let him come over tonight and fuck her brains out! And what the fuck can I do?? Nothing. I can't do shit about it. My boy was seeing her first so technically I'm in the fucking wrong. But still…I've fucked up and fallen in love with this woman. I'm just praying that she's going to tell him no or doesn't answer her phone but I know that of all nights, this is the one night that she can't get away with not speaking to him.

Shit. I need another drink. "Bartender! Give me another shot...make that two more shots of Patron!" My feelings are so hurt but let me text her to let her know that he's trying to come over there and that I don't want her to answer his calls.

(Texting her now)...

And to make matters worse, I just left her house a few hours ago. We just got through fucking and the possibility of her about to fuck him...ugh. The thought of that shit is making me sick. But at least he's going in after me but that doesn't make me feel any better. I'm taking my two shots now...hold tight for a minute.

(Few minutes later)... Thanks for waiting. I needed those shots! Anyway, I guess she's going to see him. I've sent her a few texts and she hasn't responded. What kind of hoe shit is that? Damn. I really can't be mad at her but I am. She knows that I love her and that I don't want her to see him again. And yes I know I'm a dumbass for falling in love with his side piece but hell her loving is good.

"I need you to take me to her house. I'm ready to go" he says. I'm trying to pretend like I didn't hear him so he says that shit again. Drunk bastard. I'm gonna try to get him to stay here at the club with me. Maybe if I mention his soon to be ugly ass wife, he may feel some type of guilt and decide not to go. "You know this is all wrong. What about your soon to be wife?"

"What about her?" he said. That shit didn't work so let me try something else. "You know that this is all wrong. I'm your best man and you want to leave your boys for a hoe? We all took our time to come down here for your bitch ass to have a good time and you want to ditch us? Man, tomorrow is the big day and…"

"Fuck that. Take me to see my girl. And she's not a motherfucking hoe. She's mine and I want to be with her before I make the biggest mistake of my life! Now take me over there or I'll walk if I have to!" he yelled. And he's drunk as hell. "Okay! You win! I will take you to see her" I said. She never text me back.

41

In the car…on the way to her home

Damn. I prayed that she didn't answer his phone call but it looks like she did. I sent her a bunch of messages and now she decides to text me back. What the fuck…the message reads:

"TOO LATE. I didn't get your texts in time. I just got off the phone with him and he said you were bringing him over. I'm so sorry…this is my last time with him since he's getting married tmrw. Don't be upset."

I'm shaking…like a piece of chicken in a bag of fucking flour. My heart is broken!!!! I think I'm going to throw up. Fuck this!! I feel like punching his ass in the throat, but I can't. I will drop his ass off and then just go back to the strip club so I can smell some pussy and drink my problems away. But tomorrow I'll be at his "so called" wedding….but I've got a big ass surprise waiting on his ass. Punk bitch.

Dickey's Big Day
(The wedding)

43

(Waking up…with a hard dick)…

“What time is it baby?” I ask her. I have a huge fucking hangover and I’m tired as hell. She wore my ass out last night, but I had to get it in before today. I’m not sure how she feels about seeing me after today because we never talked about it. But I think she thought that I would call the wedding off. I wish I could and she’s worth me leaving my fiancé, but I don’t want to hurt my soon to be wife.

“It’s 1 o’clock” she replied. Shit. I’m running late for my own damn wedding. I’ve got to get out of here. I’m jumping out of her bed now and headed to the shower. Damn. My wedding starts at 5 pm so I have four hours to get there. I just need to take a quick shower to make sure my dick smells fresh. My fiancé always smells my dick and balls whenever she can get a chance so trust me…she’s gonna smell them.

(10 minutes later…looking at my phone while I'm getting dressed)

Damn. I can't believe that I've got 15 missed calls and not one of them is from my best man. What the fuck? He of all people should've been calling or coming over here to get me. What the fuck does he think a best man is for? Shit. But it's my fiancé whose been calling and I don't know what to say to her but I better call her back. I know she's panicking.

(Calling my fiancé)…

"Babe, I'm on my way right now. I'm so sorry. I had a rough night last night"…I tell her but I can hear it in her voice that she's pissed off but yet worried at the same time. She just asked me where I've been all night and I told her that "I've been with my girlfriend all night! I'm just kidding. I got drunk and passed out at Harry's place. But baby I'm on the way to get dressed and will head over to the church. I won't be late. Please don't panic!"

But while my fiancé is on the phone talking, my side piece is laying across her bed fingering herself. Damn. I can't help but to watch her and my dick is getting hard all over again but I gots to go. I have to leave and get married. I'm in love with her but unfortunately I can't be with her.

Delilah and I just met at the wrong time. It's just so hard to leave her, but I've got to get my ass out of here. So I asked her to stop masturbating and even though I want to fuck her one more time, I can't. I have to leave now. But she stopped masturbating and right now she's hugging me. I'm telling her how much I love her and that I will be back for her…then I licked her fingers. I'm out.

Best man's thoughts
Wedding day
(Harry)

Driving over to D's house

(Frustrated)…I'm on my way to pick his dumb ass up for his wedding and even though I'm pissed off with her, she's all I can think about. The way that she kisses and makes love to me is just...man hands down, just the best in my life. Hmm…I wonder if she makes him feel like that or does she give him head like…?

Damn…I can't get this image of him fucking my woman out of my head but I have to. I can't keep torturing myself about this. The night is over and she promised me that she won't see him again.

I love her though and I can't help it. Sometimes I feel guilty about getting involved with her because she was with my brother first (yes he's my brother), but when I met her I just knew that she had to be mine. (smiling) I just smile thinking about when I met her for the very first time.

****Reminiscing Alert*Reminiscing Alert****

On this particular night, Thursday to be exact because of football in the middle of the week, my brother and I went out to the bar. We both like to hang out but for someone who is getting married, he doesn't act like it. But hey…that's a grown ass man and I let grown folks do what grown folks do.

Soooo while we were at the bar drinking and having a good time watching the game, he tells me that he wants to talk to me about something. He went on and said that he's not happy about getting married but he's going to go through with it anyway.

He also said that he didn't want to hurt her like that, but he had another issue going on. "What is it man? You're not gay or sick or some crazy shit like that huh?" I asked him. He shook his head and told me no but what he did share was kind of a shock.

49

My brother told me that he had met this woman and he had fallen in love with her. “I tried to fight it man but the more time that I’ve gotten to know her and spent time with her and her kids, my feelings grew deeper.”...he explained. And then of course he started to talk about their sex life and how she was “the best” that he had EVER had.

I really didn’t know what to tell him except “Bro...you sound like you’re pussy whipped.” So we continued drinking and then he said to me “I want you to meet her.” He ended up calling her and persuaded her to come up to the bar and have a few drinks with us. About an hour later, this gorgeous woman walks through the first set of doors.

I saw her before she walked completely into the building. She had on this long white fitting skirt with some heels on and a white low cut tank top on. Her skin was so brown and smooth and her skin literally glowed. The closer that she came to me, the more I wanted her. Her face was so damn beautiful and her lips...so small but yet so luscious.

At that very moment, I saw her on her knees giving me the best head of my life until she walked up to my brother and then I realized that this was the woman that he just told me about. Wow!!! "This is Delilah." he said. Her name should be Delightful.

And right then and there I knew that I was in trouble. I knew at that very moment that she and I would be lovers. So she decided to sit in between my brother and I at the bar. I was so nervous that it was hard to hide it but I did.

There I was with this woman who was the most beautiful being that I've seen in my life and she was seeing my brother. Damn. What the fuck? Here I am with no one and my brother has two women. One woman looks like a horse and the side piece looks like a Goddess. I can see why he's in love.

51

Anyway to make this short, as the night went on, she got a little tipsy and then she began to flirt with me. At first I tried to ignore the touching that she was doing because I thought that my brother noticed, but he was so fucked up that he didn't pay us any attention.

Then he went to the restroom and that's when she slipped me her business card. I put the card in my pocket and she told me to use it…soon. She then smiled and winked at me. I told her that I would call her as soon as possible. She said she was leaving and going back home. "Care to join me?" she asked.

I didn't get a chance to answer her because my brother came back from the restroom. She politely told him that she was tired and that she needed to go home…by herself to rest. They both got up from the bar and she hugged me. She whispered in my ear, "I want you" and then she let me go. My brother walked her out only to come back and have a couple of more drinks.

His fiancé finally called for him to come home so that's when we decided to leave. He asked me how I felt about his side piece but I told him that we would talk about her later. I was having thoughts about fucking her but I couldn't share that with him. He's in love…old ass sucker. LOL!

"Cool…see you later man. The soon to be wifey wants me home" he pitifully said while getting into his car. We said good bye and I watched him drive away. He wasn't out the parking lot one whole minute when I whipped out her business card and gave her a call.

"Hello", she said sounding like a sweet chocolate marshmallow bunny (whatever that sounds like I would imagine it would sound like her). "I want to see you…now" I told her. And then she gave me the directions to her house. In about 15 minutes I was there…at her home…with her lips...as I thought…wrapped perfectly…around my dick.

(Reminiscing is over…back to his wedding day)…

So that's how I got hooked up with her. And I fell in love with her just like my brother did. I couldn't help it…damn. She's really all of that but now I want her for myself. But it's okay…last night was his last night with…my future wife.

(Just arrived to her house...in her driveway...honking my horn)...

So now I'm here picking up his dumb ass to take him to his house and to the church for his wedding. He's like mega late but I wasn't going to call him. That's his dumb ass. But I've spoken to my lady on the phone and we've cleared everything up. I had to let her know that the shit that went down last night is the last time that she will be with him.

I can't take her seeing him or anyone else. We both agreed that today will be the day that we make our relationship official and known. **(Smirking)...** Yeah…I can't wait to see his face…when he realizes that the woman that he truly loves…is with me at his reception.

Please forgive me...my post is unusually long today but I'm getting dressed...I've got a wedding to go to!

(Smoking a cigarette and trying to find something to wear)…

I'm a fucking hot mess right now!!! I am sooooo nervous about going to his wedding today but his brother and I both agreed that this would be the perfect way to let his brother know that we are seeing each other.

We both know that if we do it this way then Dickey can't say anything since he will be newly married. I mean what is he going to do...confront him at the wedding? Fight his brother in front of his new wife??? (Smiling…and taking a drag from my cigarette)…

55

Anyway, I just found the perfect dress to wear to the wedding. It's all white (by now you should know that I love the color white) and it's very fitting. My clothes wouldn't be right if they didn't fit real tight is my motto.

It's low cut in the front but not too much to get too much attention. The dress is also not very long but not very short. It's very well…I would say wedding appropriate. And I guess I will wear my devil red heels!

I just can't wait to see the look on his face when Dickey sees me there. I think that's going to be enough for him to kill me but when he visually sees me with his brother…at the reception…as a couple…together…I really think that would be enough for him to go kill himself.

(Phone ringing)…

Shit. My phone rings all the damn time. I don't have time to answer it and I don't feel like answering it but I should. I know it's my baby…he's probably letting me know that he's dropped the soon to be groom off and he's waiting on me to arrive. So let me answer this phone…

"Hello darling!" I said and I can't help but to smile. I didn't bother to look at the caller id…but he's speaking and it's not who I thought it was. So he's saying a lot and I really don't want to ask who the hell it is so I just listen…waiting to catch his voice.

57

And right when he said, “I can’t wait to see you at the wedding. You know I’ll be there with my wife but I just want to see you since I can’t hold you.”…it hit me like a ton of bricks on my head….fuck it. It’s their **father!!!!** Yes…theirs.

I can’t do this today…I really can’t. “I …uhh…umm…yeah can’t wait to see you as well but I ummm…need to go.” I said to him and hung up. Damn it! I totally forgot about him. I so forgot that he was in the equation. Damn. Well I need to get dressed. Bye.

Delilah

Papa Dickey's Thoughts (Quick and meaningless)...

59

(In the mirror…trying to tie this damn tie)…

It's my son's wedding day today and I'm trying to get dressed right now but my wife is running around here like a chicken with its damn head cut off. I'm thankful for that because it gives me time to make my phone call. So let me call Delilah right now. My heart is beating so damn fast and I hope that she answers. (She answers and greets me with "Hello darling!") I know that she still wants me.

She seems to be so excited to hear my voice right now that I'm telling her that I miss her so much. We both will be attending Dickey's wedding (I invited her) but I hope to see her later on tonight. I didn't want anyone to know about her but I ended up introducing her to Dickey…by default. He actually caught us together so I had to spill the beans to him. So he's the only one that knows.

Anyway, she's my heart. I tried not to fall for her but this has been very difficult for me. I know I love her and well…it's complicated. I love my wife but we haven't made love in years. And Delilah…well she's the next best thing to peanut butter and jelly. **(smiling)…**And she's the best I've ever had…in all my sexual years.

Just thinking about her makes me smile and makes my dick jump for JOY! (She's telling me that she has to go for now)…The great news is that she's going to try to fit me in her schedule. I'll just text her to let her know that I'm always thinking about her. I'm just ready to go so I can spend time with….
"You ready Dick?" my wife yells as she interrupts my fucking thoughts. I have to go now… "I'm ready dear."

I don't know about you but right now can you say, "Speechless!" Damn I didn't know that he has such strong feelings for me. I hate to sound so cold but the sex with Papa Dickey was meaningless to me. It was something that just fucking happened. I had a lot of fun with their dad and he will always be someone memorable in my life, but for real?

Of all days to call me! I just hope that he doesn't choke up when he sees me at the wedding. But more importantly I hope he doesn't have a heart attack or stroke when he sees me at his reception…dancing…with his young son. Damn. I haven't spoken to his old ass in like…forever. (Sighing)…Sorry folks…it's something about them damn 3's.

Two brothers and their dad…it can be a little too much. But it gets a little tricky. Soooo…one brother knows about the other brother but the other brother doesn't know about the young brother and well…the one brother knows about me and their father but the other have no fucking idea that I was seeing their father. And the father…we he's clueless…he doesn't quite know about me seeing his sons. Confused? Yes me too…I'll get back with you on that later. But right now I need to leave.

Delilah.

The weak off
Nigel

(In the bathroom)…

Give me just a few minutes to gather my thoughts. Right now I'm sitting on the toilet and I'm getting my dick sucked right now. You can't possibly believe that I would have any other thoughts about anything except…getting my dick sucked.

(20 minutes later)…

Okay…she sucked me off and I feel like a fucking winner!!! And on top of all of that, she swallowed my cum and now her ass is downstairs cooking me some motherfucking breakfast!!! She said, "Big daddy…I'm gonna serve you breakfast in bed!" Yeah…being the king that I am, I'm in her bed chilling while she's cooking and I want some more of that sweet ass.

65

(Laying in her bed…with my hands behind my head)…

I'm about to cum just thinking about her. She is so fucking good…scratch that thought! She's fucking great!!!! Not just her sex…but her…the person. Period. I love her attitude. She's so funny and just fun to be around. And she's so damn fine…I just can't get over how fine she is. Funny and fine as hell.

She's brown skinned with the prettiest smile you will ever see. And her lips…boyyyyyyyyyy! Her lips are small but yet so tender. The feel of her lips wrapped around my dick…awwwww damn…I'm getting on hard. Hmmmm…And the way that she kisses my balls. Fan-fucking-tastic!

I feel like screaming and I need more of her but I'm going to be patient. Like I said, my queen is cooking her king a hot ass breakfast…like that hot ass pussy she's got between her thighs. And she's been cooking for me and fucking me all week longgggggggggggg!!!! Yessssss…my best week **EVER!**

I can't believe that she took a whole week off from her job just to be with me. Damn…makes me feel special but hell I took the week off to be with her so she's pretty special in my book. But unfortunately I have to go back to work tonight. I'm gonna ask her if she wants to go with me to meet my friends. I want to show her off to the boys so they can see how I roll. Hold up for a minute…she's yelling at me from downstairs.

Okay…she told me that she's made me some homemade blueberry waffles, cheese eggs, bacon and cheese grits. Damn. And we are going to eat each other…I meant eat breakfast in bed. It's hard getting her out of my head…and out of bed. (Smiling)…I love her.

(Phone buzzing)…

Who the fuck is texting me this time of the morning? Shit…I know it's not the job and it better not be that sorry ass motherfuc…

67

(Picking up the phone and reading the text)....

Damnit! I can't believe this is happening. (Sighing)...Okay she just walked in with breakfast so I can't trip. We're about to get our eat on and I can't let her see me stressed out. The cool part about her is that she never ever asks me any questions about who calls my phone or anything. Like right now, she saw me reading my text and she didn't ask who called or sent me a text. She just brought the food in and didn't say anything.

That's why I love her. She treats me like a king and she gives me my space. And she has the best sex that I've ever had. And she's a good mother. She loves her kids and that's another reason why I can't let her go. She's a good woman. But anyway, let me eat breakfast with my honey bun. I'll be back.

(About 45 minutes later, after we've eaten)…

She's lying in my arms right now and as much as I want to have sex with her, I really feel good just knowing that she's in my arms. Someday I want to be with her…just me and her…just us. She's my Bonnie and I'm going to be her Clyde.

Right now I can't give her what she needs from me. That phone call that I got…I have to leave her for a little while but I want her to know that I'm coming back. But I can't be all that she needs and deserves because at this very moment, **my wife is in the hospital giving birth to my son**.

What the fuck do I do now?

MY WIFE IS IN LABOR AND I STILL HAVEN'T LEFT HER HOUSE...I'M WHIPPED.COM
NIGEL

(Out of her bed and in the shower washing my balls)…

I hate that I have to leave her. This has been a great week but I've to check on my wife and our soon to be newborn son. (Shaking my head)…I know. I feel really bad and I should've told her that I was married but I'm scared.

I don't want to lose her, but I'm not sure if this is the right time to tell her. And I don't know how she's going to handle me being married as well as my wife and I having a baby on the way. I'm pretty sure that she's going to leave me.

(I hear her voice…her sweet voice that matches her sweet stuff that's in between her thighs)

"Baby where are you?" …She's calling me and I just want to hold her. "I'm getting out of the shower" I yelled.

71

(Out of the shower…getting dressed)…

I'm rushing out so that I can talk to her about me leaving, but I don't know what to really tell her. I mean do I tell her the truth or do I continue to lie to her? I'm really scared.

I didn't think that I would fall for her at all. I mean I just met her like 4 weeks ago at a club and I thought that I would just hit it and leave but damn. Here I am lying to my wife about where I am and not wanting to be with my wife because of her. Shit! But I can't leave my wife, not now. But let me talk to Delilah and continue the lies.

(I'm talking to her now and I feel worse lying to her than to my own wife…but I gotta do what I gotta do!)

She just told me she will be here when I return and that my business is mine. I'm smiling at her right now…and my heart wants to tell her that I'm going to hospital to be with my wife because she's having our baby. But before I could say anything else, she has pushed me down on the bed and she's now sucking my dick again….hold tight.

Damn…

I just came in her mouth again and we fucked for another hour. I'm telling her that I have to leave but I will be back soon. I can't bear the thought of losing her so I chose to lie…and tell her that my job needed me to come in for another guy.

(Shrugging my shoulders)…

Sorry…I can't do this right now…I can't lose her because I love her…more than I love my own wife. I'm dressed now and headed out. She's hugging me right now and I kiss her on her neck and tell her that I'll be back for her. I don't want to leave but …I just don't know when. Damn.

Personally, from me to you, I'm just fucking glad that he's gone. Whoever called him, which I know was his wife, I could kiss their feet. And I know he's married. And yes I know he's having a kid. Let me get a cigarette and explain something to you about me. Hold tight…

(Lighting my cigarette)…

Mama didn't raise a fool. I am very educated although I'm very liberated in my sexual appetite. But being that I'm no one's fool, I checked his arse (that is not a typo…I use that for the word **ass**) out a couple of weeks ago. He came over here one night and he came and came and finally he went to sleep.

And I'll let you figure out the rest. It's not that very complicated….I gathered my information from his cell phone and made contact with his wife. I didn't call and spill the beans on him.

Why would I cut my nose off in spite of my face?? Hell, he's fine as hell and he's hung and more importantly I'm at peace with the whole shituation. But I did visit her. Yeah I told him that I had to go to the store, but what he didn't know is I went to her photography studio and had a photo session with her.

When he gets back, I will have a nice butt naked
ass picture of myself waiting on him…with her portrait signature in the bottom right hand corner that says "Jackson 2011". Sorry Ms. Jackson. (Their last name).

(Phone ringing)…Be right back.

Delilah.

Uncle Bobby

The family outing

(On the boat)…

Right now I'm out on the lake driving my new boat. I've got my friends and family with me, but more importantly I have her on the boat. She is so sexy to me that the mere thought of her makes my dick rise. Look at her over there sitting down, sipping on her wine and talking to her girlfriend.

(Smiling as the wind is hitting my face)…

She's so beautiful and young. She's wearing this long white dress that looks like a halter top dress or something. Hell I'm not a fashion expert but I know one thing for sure…she's fine as hell. I wish I could just stop this boat, kick everyone off including my wife and make love to her but I can't.

Anyway, we're enjoying this nice holiday and she just came up to me and said that she wish that I could teach her how to drive my boat. My dick is harder than a rock but I must look like I'm in control but I want to suck her nipples…I'm just saying.

"Well someday I will let you ride my (I want to say dick)…boat! No problem! As long as you promise me one thing…" I said to her. "What's that?" she says to me. "Come back in about 15 minutes and I will tell you what that is."

She said okay and walked away. I wish I could turn around and watch her walk away. She looks good coming and going, but I can't get distracted from this boat. I don't want to crash while thinking about licking her ass cheeks. (Smiling)…

(30 minutes later and we are back on land)…

"What's the promise?"…she said as she sneaked up on me. "The promise?" I said. Somehow I forgot but hell I am 70 years old. Damn. "Oh yes…the promise! Oh…I remember now. "Can you come with me for a few minutes? Everyone else is having fun so they won't miss us." I said. "Sure" she replied and we walked to the balcony which overlooked the lake.

(A few minutes later…we're in my car and she's giving me the best head that I've had in my life…Give me about 5 more minutes so I can finish this…)

Okay she just finished me off and now I'm okay to talk to her. So in the heat of the moment, I asked her to always care about me. What the fuck? I'm 70 not 7.

Shit I've got to get myself together. Right now she's saying something but I'm not paying her any attention besides just watching her. She's just so fucking gorgeous. I feel like a young man again. And the way that she made love to me last night, she had me wide open.

I've got to give her credit…she's the best fuck I have ever had. I know that there's some type of prize for her to win. She should win the "best fuck award". But what's scary about this whole situation is the fact that I've fallen in love with her and I couldn't help it.

(5 minutes passes away and she lets me know that we need to go back...inside...with the rest of the family)...

As she's turning away from me, I couldn't help but to ask her to promise me that she won't leave me and to love me back. She's not answering me and now she's walking way. I'm not really sure but maybe she left because my wife (who has a knife in her hand) is standing in my window crying. Or maybe because she's my nephew's fiancé? I don't know what to think at this point. "What the fuck have I gotten myself into?" is the only thing that comes to my mind right now.

Really? Seriously? I can't believe that his old ass asked this of me. I mean how in the hell do I not supposed to care and fall in love with his nephew? His nephew is a wonderful guy but he did make a good argument about two things: his nephew is broke and he's really not worth shit.

(Smiling)... That's not the point though. Anyway I'm not trying to get married to anyone let alone his nephew. But really...if his old ass only knew that I didn't give a shit about his nephew. And I thought the proof was in the pudding. Shouldn't the old man look at my actions? I mean I am fucking him and his nephew. So if I actually gave a shit, wouldn't I be faithful? Something to think about...it's not that hard.

One more thing...I don't know but although the sex with his 70 year old uncle is great, there's something a little off with his ass. It seems at some point, in my opinion, that when you are about 70 then you shouldn't be snorting cocaine. And the fact that he bought a dildo...in which he made me use it on him. Maybe it's me...I'm just saying.

Oh yeah, I forgot to tell you that his wife…well she was crying with the knife because she was cutting onions. Yeah I peeped that when I went outside to give her husband some head in the car. She was cooking as usual and she didn't know what the hell happened. The onions made her cry.

Side story: once I went back into the house, well the old man's grandson, who is 3, ran up and jumped in my arms. But before I could stop him…well let's just say he pecked me on the lips…and got a little taste of grandpa…on his. ☺

Delilah.

Uncle Tommy...The family outing part 2

(On the boat with my family)…

I'm with my family right now out on the lake and it's a beautiful day. I'm chilling with my wife and of course my nephew decides to bring his fine ass fiancé and her ugly ass friend to the celebration.

I wonder if he's serious about this one? My nephew is whorish and he's brought around some whorish ass women, but I don't know…this one seems to be different. She's smart, sexy and well she's not my wife let me just say that.

Anyway, we're up here for the weekend since it's a holiday. I had to bring my wife with me because she's always bitching about how she never gets to travel with me and besides she wanted to see her sister so who the fuck am I to deny her. But she is ruining my chances for me to talk to my nephew's new girlfriend.

85

(Sipping on my beer...thinking about the last time I came to Georgia)....

I came up here about 3 weeks ago on a business trip and I got a chance to spend a little time with my family up here without my wife. And that's when I met my nephew's new girlfriend.

We were all chilling at the lake house that my brother-in-law owns and my nephew walks in with one of the finest ass females that I've seen in my life! She was so damn fine that my dick got on hard…immediately.

Anyway, my nephew's new girlfriend was wearing these tight white jeans with this sheer white shirt and these heels that made me want to holler but I couldn't. Her skin was so brown and smooth like cocoa that at that very moment when I saw her, I knew I had to have her.

I knew that I was wrong for that but I couldn't help it. At that moment I saw myself fucking her from the back. And then I was on top of her with her big thighs wrapped around my waist. Hmmmm…yes I decided at that very moment that I was going to fuck her.

I also knew that I needed to pray because I was going to be in trouble with my nephew's girl. And believe it or not, I didn't give a shit. I didn't know what I had to do to get her, but I knew that I was going to have that chocolate morsel…even if it killed me to get her.

So, as the night progressed, we as in the family, partied hard all night long. We literally partied until the next morning but unfortunately for my nephew he didn't last. His sorry ass was knocked the fuck out but not his girl… oh noooo…not Miss Sexual Hot Chocolate.

She was still up…sitting on the patio…drinking her beer while she was watching the sunrise. And they both were beautiful. I just wanted to grab her and eat her up but that was all in my head. She's probably so committed to him that she doesn't even look at another man in his eyes without him.

But I decided to throw caution in the wind and I figured that this would be my opportunity to talk to her…to get more acquainted with her. I mean there's a possibility that someday she just might be a part of this family so I felt that it was my duty as his uncle to check out how her loyalty to him. So I went out on the patio to talk to her to see where her head was at.

"Good morning to you" I said. "Morning! How are you?" she replied. I really wanted to tell her that I wanted to take her to the backroom and fuck her from the back but that wouldn't have been appropriate. (chuckle) "I see that you had a good time last night" I said. And she said that she had a great evening.

After we got all of the preliminaries out the way and we both realized that my nephew and everyone in the house was knocked the fuck out and the small fact that my wife was not here, out of the blue she blurted out, **"I'm horny as hell!"**

"Where in the hell did that come from?" I asked. "You've been checking me out since the moment you've met me. And I've been feeling the same way about you. So now the only thing that's standing between us is air and opportunity so what are you going to do?" she said and then she guzzled the rest of her beer.

I knew she was drunk and I was still drinking but damn. I wasn't expecting that to come out of her mouth. "What about my nephew?" I whispered to her as my dick began to rise with the sun. "What about him? He's knocked out and I'm not his girlfriend. He's seeing other people and I am too. And right now I want to see you…naked…and inside of me. I want to fuck. So what are you going to do?"

And I did what any other man in their right mind would have done in my situation. I mean damn. I am loyal to my nephew and I can’t believe that this is the type of woman that he would want in our family.

So being the man that I am… I politely took her downstairs where there was an empty bathroom and did what her man should’ve done. I fucked the hell out of her!!! (You didn’t think I was that stupid did ya! I mean damn…I couldn’t pass up on an opportunity like that.) And besides that, my dumbass nephew shouldn’t have ever left her alone.

He’s the fool! And I just couldn’t say no to her. She did say that she was horny and I felt as if it was my duty to fulfill her needs at the moment. She told me that her pussy was throbbing and that she needed me.

And for the record, she was amazing. I just couldn't pass up on this opportunity to be with her. The way that she sucked my dick while I sat on the edge of the tub was spectacular. And she let me cum in her mouth!!! I've never experienced that before.

But surprisingly after I came in her mouth, I got hard again and fucked her from the back while she was bent over the sink. That was a fantastic experience!!! So I came to the decision that my nephew must not see her again because she's a hoe…a good hoe. But I wanted to keep her for myself!

91

(Back to reality and back on land)…

Yeah that's how we met. I'm sitting across from her and I wish I could talk to her but my wife is watching me like a hawk. But I did get a chance to send her a text earlier. I told her that I want to see her again and that she should be expecting a round trip ticket from me pretty soon. She said she would be obliged! She also wrote that "she wants me to cum in her mouth again!" Whewwwweeee!! I'll drink to that!

Cheers!

Mini-vacation~
Not many thoughts

93

(In the hotel room, watching my lovely girlfriend on the patio overlooking the river)….

She's the love of my life...the apple of my eye and I don't know what life would be without her. I am so in love with her that my heart hurts sometimes. Right now we are in Savannah on vacation and we've been dating for almost 5 years.

We are at this beautiful hotel which overlooks the river and as she stands on the balcony, I can't help but to stare at how beautiful she is. She's wearing a white mini dress just for me to look at her legs. She has the prettiest legs I've ever seen and I just want to kiss them.

We just got through making love and as usual, it felt like paradise. She always knows how to touch me in the right spot and her kisses are like silk. By the way, she gives the best blow job that I've ever had in my life. I am so in love with her it's ridiculous.

Now she's walking back in the hotel and she's saying how much she loves me. I love you too baby! **(Blowing kisses at her)** I am so fucking weak for this woman that it's insane. (sigh) If I could give her the world I would, but all I can give her is me and my soul.

This woman is phenomenal. (She's speaking right now....) Okay she just reminded me that it's time to pack up our shit and get going because check out is at 12 noon. But it feels so fucking good to be alone with my girl....which is rare. This is our first real vacation but it won't be our last. In a couple of months, I'm going to take her to Paris…for some shopping.

I want to ask her to marry me…but I have an issue right now. "Time to go!" she yelled. And reality has set in. It's time for me to go home….**to my wife of 27 years...who also happens to be her mother. (DON'T JUDGE ME!)** Long story…don't want to talk about it nor think about that shit! And yes I'm in love with her and I'm going to continue to see her.

I have pondered over this situation and I'm glad that he didn't give any more thoughts or recollections about our relationship. I've seen enough and I'm sure that you have too. But I have come to the conclusion that in this situation there are no excuses. There's nothing to justify our actions and to be honest, I'm not trying to justify anything.

Unless my mother picks up this book and figures out that I slept with her husband, then there's no excuses needed. But if she picks this book up and she realizes that it's me that did that to her husband (trust me…I did things to him) then I will offer one of the 5 excuses which works for almost anything. The following top 5 excuses are:

5. You didn't raise me/I didn't live with you.
4. He's a lie. I wouldn't do that to you.
3. What type of proof do you have?
2. He told me that he wasn't married.
1. Better me than some stranger off the street.

Delilah.

The big head baby...

(Walking into the room)…

Wow. There goes the woman of my dreams. She's laying there in the hospital bed wrapped up in a white sheet. She also has on an oxygen mask and machines are hooked up to her as if she's dying. But she's not dying…she's giving birth to our son. (The doctor comes in and he's asking me to step outside the door for a few minutes)…I kiss her forehead and I leave. (In the hall)…I've never been so scared in my life.

I can't stand to look at her in that much pain and there's nothing that I can do about it. Shit! (sigh) I have to trust in God that she and our baby will be alright. **(Doctor pokes his head out and tells me that I can come back in the room)** I whispered to her "I'm back" just to let her know that I'm here for both of them. But she's in a lot of pain right now.

(Beep, Beep)...I'm hearing this beeping and I turn to look at the machine and the lines on here are going wild. I have to go get the doctor because I don't know what the fuck is going on. (**Running out of the room)....**

The doctor is with them now. I'm in the hallway all by myself and I need a cigarette but more importantly I need a plan. I'm so confused right now that it hurts. We don't even have a name for our son and she doesn't have a job. Well she has a job but it's just not a good paying job right now. She delivers pizza but she doesn't make that much money doing that.

So it's apparent that I'll be the supporter of our child, but that's not an issue right now. I just want both of them to make it through this!!! I'm so fucking nervous that I'm sweating. My underarms are wet as piss and it's nothing that I can do. Damn. Let me go…the doctor is calling me back into the room.

99

(Speaking to the doctor)…

(sigh)…The doctor just told me that both of them are stable now. They found out that my son wasn't breathing properly inside of her and they had to do something to help him out. What the fuck? But they are fine now. I'm just ready for her to have him and get this over with. (She screams) I'm going back into the room now.

(2 hours later)….All I hear is screaming and now I hear crying…(I'm in tears)…my son is here. She just gave birth to our son. He's 6 pounds 8 ounces but his **head is big as fuck**! Damn! But the doctors cleaned him up and I get to be the first one to hold him. Bring him to papa!!!

(Holding our son and in tears)...

I just told her that no matter what happens that I will always love them. But she's looking at me as if she wants to shoot me or something so I'm walking away from her. Besides that, the nurses are getting her cleaned up and I'm still holding our son.

(Looking down smiling at my son...)

He's so handsome. I love him already. (Nurses leave)...They are finished with her and we've finally decided on his name and I can't be more thrilled but still nervous at the same time.

101

(Tap on my shoulder)…

The doctor just asked me to leave because they are taking her out of the room. I hand over our son to her so she can hold him and I kissed her on the lips…softly. “I love the both of you.” I said to them. And now she’s gone. I’m leaving the hospital right now but I need to think.

(Left the hospital and sitting in my car smoking a cigarette)…

What the fuck do I do now? This is all fucked up. I already have a little girl and a 2 year old son. Now this? Ughh…I mean I’m happy to have another child but not now…not like this. I’m fucked up right now because I want to do the right thing by her but what but more importantly how in the fuck am I going to tell my **wife**?

My thoughts:

Fuck him....

I mean there's nothing else to really say at this point. Not because he's married, but because…well I will save that story for later.

until the next time...

Delilah.

Disclaimer:

"We at BetrayalBooks.com pride ourselves on being able to betray everyone including our readers.

We appreciate you reading this book and we look forward to betraying you again!"

His Thoughts, Her Thoughts... Volume 1.5 (Conclusions) coming soon!

P.S.

This book was self-published and we apologize for any inconsistencies with this book such as the page numbers might have been out of place or other small nuances that didn't affect the story.

Again we apologize. We at BetrayalBooks.com are doing our best to make sure that our future books are well…damn. I can't even say this right. Okay well we hope that you enjoyed the book and to hell with the errors. We will do better once we get a big publisher to buy us out. (Hey, we've done our best though.)

But thank you for reading this book and we hope that you enjoyed the stories. If you are on Facebook and you really enjoyed this book, please go to our page His Thoughts, Her Thighs and like us. If you are on Twitter, please follow us at #BetrayalBooks.com. And if you may be interested in purchasing our books in bulk at a discount, please contact us at www.BetrayalBooks.com.

We appreciate your business.

Made in the USA
Columbia, SC
12 November 2024

46178849R00065